MY BROTHER IS A
ROBOT

BOOK 2

THE MASTER PLAN

AMANDA RONAN

The Master Plan
My Brother is a Robot #2

Copyright © 2016

Published by Scobre Educational

Written by Amanda Ronan

Scobre Educational
2255 Calle Clara
La Jolla, CA 92037

Scobre Operations & Administration
42982 Osgood Road
Fremont, CA 94539

www.scobre.com
info@scobre.com

Scobre Educational publications may be purchased for
educational, business, or sales promotional use.

Cover and layout design by Nicole Ramsay
Copyedited by Kristin Russo

ISBN: 978-1-62920-498-7 (Library Bound)
ISBN: 978-1-62920-497-0 (eBook)

For Casey and Lamar, the world's cutest pups.

Scooter's got nothing on you two.

CHAPTER 1

MY FINGERS GRIPPED THE PENCIL TIGHTLY AS I STRUGGLED to come up with the next sentence in my essay. Through the window, I saw my friend James playing basketball with some of the other kids in the neighborhood, including my brother, Cyrus.

"This is so stupid. Nobody uses pencils to write anymore!" I tossed my pencil at the window. The plunking sound made Scooter, my lazy Basset Hound, open one eye. When he didn't see any food around,

Scooter quickly lost interest and went back to snoozing on Cyrus's pile of laundry.

The essay was due Monday and I'd been working on it all week. I wasn't being a nerd or anything; I just had nothing else to do while I was grounded. See, about a month ago, Cyrus did my homework for me and I got caught cheating and kicked off the basketball team. My parents grounded me for two months—no phone, no computer, no video games, no friends, and absolutely no fun. I was only halfway through with my punishment and was starting to go a little crazy.

"Hey, Shawn?" My mom poked her head into my room. She was wearing her white lab coat, which wasn't unusual for a Saturday morning. Mom was a mechanical engineer who loved her job. She didn't believe in leaving work at the office. In fact, her work was living with us. My brother Cyrus, who looked just like me, was a robot. He was one of my mom's projects. "How's the essay?"

I turned to face her. "Bad."

"Why's that?" She stepped into my room. She looked tiny next to my life-sized poster of Shaquille O'Neal.

"Because I can't write a whole paper in my notebook. My hand is cramping." I flexed my fingers to show her how much pain I was in. "Besides, the essay has to be typed. It's in the directions. Can I please have my laptop back?" I stuck out my bottom lip, hoping a pouty face might help my cause.

My mom crossed her arms in front of her. "That is a very sad story, Shawn. But, no. You're grounded. Rules are rules."

"Fine." I turned back to my desk.

My mom walked across the room and sat on my bed. "I wanted to let you know that Cyrus and I will be working downstairs and things might get a little distracting."

"Whatever," I mumbled. I wasn't surprised she

was going to spend the day with Cyrus. Since she'd brought him home, she'd barely spent any time with me. They were always working in her office, sharing stupid science jokes, and talking about things that I can't even spell.

She stood and put her hands on my shoulders. "Okay, well, just thought I'd warn you. We're going to do some testing on Cyrus's emotional responses to unpleasant stimuli. I thought I'd try to get this done before your dad gets back. You know how he feels about my working with Cyrus at home." She kissed the top of my head and left the room.

I heard her go downstairs and call Cyrus in from the basketball game.

"Emotional responses to unpleasant stimuli . . . " I said in voice mimicking my mom. I turned to Scooter. "What does that even mean?"

I found out a few minutes later, when a bloodcurdling scream rang out from downstairs. At first my brain didn't make sense of what was going on. So I went back to writing my essay. A few minutes later though, another scream was quickly followed by three more and I couldn't ignore it any longer.

I burst through the lab door and adjusted my eyes to the dark. There was a flat screen mounted to the wall showing a video of a giggling baby. Cyrus was watching the video and screaming like he was being trampled by a rhinoceros. When he saw me standing in the doorway, he stopped screaming and smiled. "Hey Shawn! I didn't think you were coming out of your room today." He looked behind me at Scooter, who was panting heavily after his slow trip down the stairs.

"What are you doing? Why are you screaming?" I asked, trying to catching my breath.

My mom looked up from her laptop. "I told you, honey, we're testing Cyrus's reactions to unpleasant stimuli."

I pointed to the screen. "But that's an adorable baby. Why is Cyrus screaming like that?"

My mom smiled. "We're just calibrating his responses."

I shook my head. "I don't know what that means."

"And you don't need to." She stood and walked over to me. She wrapped an arm around my shoulder and walked me back through the door. "What you need to do is go upstairs and finish your essay on the Civil War."

"But, is Cyrus going to scream like that all afternoon?" I looked over her shoulder and watched him sitting on the stool. He was dangling his legs back and forth like he was having a great time.

"Probably not, no. I'm working on programming appropriate responses to things he sees. He needs to know what he should scream at and what he should laugh at. Get it?"

I nodded.

"You tell us if we're being too loud, okay?" She tossed me a pair of headphones. "Use these, they're noise-cancelling."

I hung the headphones around my neck and wondered where my mom got such cool accessories. I looked down at Scooter. "Okay, Scoot, back upstairs."

He looked at me once and then walked in the opposite direction, too tired to bother joining me.

When I got back upstairs I heard a knock at the front door. Thinking Mom would get it, I sat down at my desk. I looked out the window and my eyes widened when I saw the car parked in our driveway. I jogged back downstairs and called, "Mom, the police are here!" before opening the door.

CHAPTER 2

"**M**A'AM, WE'RE HERE BECAUSE OF A NOISE COMPLAINT. I'm Officer Sanders and this is Officer Gregson. Is everything all right?"

My mom laughed. "Of course, officers. Please come in."

They stepped into the living room and looked around. Officer Sanders looked at me. "Anything wrong, son? Were you just screaming?"

I shook my head and decided to let my mom deal with this mess.

Cyrus walked out of the office and stood behind the couch, eyeing the police officers.

"What about you, son? Were you making all that noise?" Then he looked back at me and immediately recognized that we looked alike. "Twins, eh?"

"Not exactly," my mother jumped in. "I'm Dr. Samira Cole from Smith and Company labs. This is our son, Shawn," she pointed at me, "and our robot son, Cyrus. You may have heard of him. He's been in the news recently."

Behind the police officers, the front door opened. "*Samira*," my dad said angrily, before he registered what was going on. He looked around the room at me and Mom and Cyrus. He smiled politely, introduced himself to policemen, and then said, "Shawn, go to your room," without looking back at me.

"But Dad—"

The look he gave me told me to not even *try* arguing with him right now.

"Cyrus, you go with him."

"But Mr. Cole—" Cyrus got the same look and we both started trudging up the stairs to my room.

———

My dad didn't say anything during dinner that night. He ate his dinner really fast and then excused himself from the table.

"Your dad is a little upset about what happened this afternoon. He'll be fine," my mom explained and stood to clear her plate. "Cyrus, would you join us in the office?"

I looked down at my plate. I still hadn't finished my spaghetti, but after seeing Dad so angry, I wasn't hungry. My dad liked things a certain way. He was a strict rule follower, so finding the police in our home was not on the top of his list of favorites. The quiet, stewing anger during dinner made me worried that something big was about to happen.

I wiped some sauce off half a meatball and tossed it

to Scooter. He swallowed it in one gulp and looked up, hoping for more. Reaching below the table, I laughed and scratched his ears. "That's all you're getting, big guy."

After cleaning up from dinner, I was supposed to go back to my room, but I thought I'd take a detour and listen to what was going on in Mom's office.

My dad's voice was clear, even though it was coming through the heavy door. "No, Samira, the neighbors aren't going to just forget what they heard. They thought someone was being attacked!"

My mom murmured a response that I couldn't hear, so I pressed my ear against the door. Scooter lay down in front of me and quickly fell into a post-meatball nap.

"We agreed that this was just a trial and my patience is running thin. How do you think I felt when I got home and saw police cars in the driveway?"

After the police checked to make sure we were safe and Mom promised to stop testing Cyrus's reactions, they agreed to leave without writing up any formal report. Dad was furious, and hadn't calmed down since then.

Mom's voice was still impossible to hear, but then Cyrus spoke up. "Mr. Cole, if I can explain . . ."

"No, Cyrus, you may not. This work you two are doing needs to stay at the lab. It's one thing for you to live here and try to act like a normal eleven-year-old boy. It's another thing to do creepy, screaming experiments in the living room!"

"We were in the office!" Mom exclaimed.

My dad sighed loudly. "That is not the point. I'll make this easy for you both. You have one week to show me that we can live like a normal family—that means no visits from the police; no waking up at three a.m. because Cyrus's security alarm is going off like it did last month; no helping our son cheat; and no experiments at home. If you can do that for a week, Cyrus can stay. If not—if anything at all goes wrong and Cyrus is involved—he's moving back to the lab."

I waited for my mom to respond, but there was silence. Instead, to my surprise, my dad tugged the door open. I fell into the room, looking guilty. "Oh, hey, I was just, um . . . "

My dad crossed his arms and looked over at Cyrus.

Cyrus held up his hands, "I was not involved in Shawn's eavesdropping. That should not count against me!"

My dad looked back down at me and frowned. "Well? Get off the floor and go to your room."

I trudged up the stairs with Scooter close behind me. I needed to talk to Cyrus. We needed to make a plan.

—————

Cyrus sat down on my bed and rubbed his head.

"You have a headache?" I asked.

He shook his head, "No, I've just seen your mom do this when she's stressed."

"So, you're feeling stressed?"

He shook his head again and said, "Not really, no. But I'm supposed to be feeling stressed, so I'm acting like it."

"You are so weird, man," I laughed.

"So, you heard everything downstairs?" Cyrus stood up and looked out the window. The sun was just setting and the streetlights were starting to buzz before they turned on.

"Yeah, we've got to figure out how to make my dad like you. You can't just go back to the lab. How will I learn all the cheat codes for Zombie Playground?"

Cyrus shrugged. "I'm not sure what we can do. Your dad definitely wants me gone and he'll be on the lookout for anything to use as an excuse to get rid of me. I don't think you can stay out of trouble for long enough to help me out here."

"What's that supposed to mean?" I laughed.

Cyrus pointed to the laptop sticking out from under a pile of folded laundry. "You're not supposed to have that, for one. What'd you do, grab it from the table while your mom was distracted by the police?"

"Well, when you put it that way it sounds bad, but, yes, I didn't think she'd notice. I need it for my essay."

"If your dad thinks I gave it to you . . . "

I grabbed the laptop. "Okay, okay. I'll put it back later. You really think there's nothing we can do to get you on my dad's good side?"

"Why? What do you think we should do?"

I thought about what made my dad happy. "He likes to go fishing. Maybe you could go with him."

Cyrus shook his head. "The slime might get into my hard drives."

"But you're waterproof . . . "

"Fine, it's the smell. I think fish are gross."

I shook my head. "Well, that's a problem. What about cooking? He loves to cook."

"Shawn, you know I can't taste food. How could I help him with that?"

I shrugged. "I dunno. Read him a recipe, make him a cookbook, and help him chop vegetables?"

Cyrus nodded. "Okay . . . maybe. What else?"

"You tell me. Can't you pull up information about my dad from all your databases? Maybe we find out about some secret talents or interests that will help us make a plan."

Cyrus blinked his eyes. "Yes."

"Well, then, do it."

"I just did."

I rolled my eyes and flipped my notebook to the back page. "Okay, tell me what you know. I'll write it down and we'll be able to figure out a plan."

"Why would you write it down? I have it stored on a memory card."

I threw my pencil at Cyrus. "Just tell me what you know—"

"Nathaniel Alvin Cole, born April 10, 1973. Married Samira Yvonne Singh after just two months of dating. They told people it was love at first sight. They shared their first kiss—"

"Ugh! Why are you telling me this?!" I quickly covered my ears.

Cyrus chuckled to himself, then he said, "Okay, I'll move on. Nathaniel Alvin Cole, part-time commodities broker, part time stay-at-home dad. He has a brown belt in Kung Fu—"

"What?!"

Cyrus nodded. "Yes, he practiced as a teenager and in college. He also spent a year backpacking around Italy and taking cooking classes. He volunteers at the animal shelter on Tuesdays and—"

"He does?" The man Cyrus was describing was

AMANDA RONAN

definitely not my dad. "I think you searched for the wrong Nathaniel Cole."

"I don't think your mom is married to two men with the same name," Cyrus said.

"Ew, again. Do you have enough to figure something out now? I don't think I want to know anymore."

Cyrus blinked. "Yes. I've made a plan."

"So what is it?" I leaned forward, prepared to be amazed.

Cyrus stood up and walked to the door. "I can't tell you. You'll ruin it."

As he shut the door behind him, I looked over at Scooter and said, "Well, that was rude."

Scooter sneezed and went back to sleep.

CHAPTER 3

"**C**YRUS, WOULD YOU PLEASE STAY AFTER CLASS?"

I looked up from my desk sharply. Our English teacher, Mrs. Cray was watching the class file out on the way to lunch. Cyrus started rearranging the paperclips in the apple-shaped dish on her desk. When I walked by I murmured, "What'd you do?"

Cyrus shrugged, not looking too concerned. When he came into the lunchroom, I waved him over. I still sat with the other guys on the basketball team, even though the coach had kicked me off for cheating. I was trying to keep my grades up and show him I was responsible. He was considering letting me join as a sub if I kept doing well.

"Yo, Cyrus, what did crabby old Cray want?" I asked. Jensen moved over so Cyrus could sit.

"She needed help fixing her computer. The school's IT department wouldn't respond to her emails and she needed to be able to log in to finish up third quarter grades." Cyrus sat and adjusted the cover on one of his fingers, under which I knew housed a Philips head screwdriver.

I leaned forward and asked, "Did you fix it?"

Cyrus tilted his head to one side. "Of course I fixed it."

I chewed my sandwich slowly as Cyrus explained something about a motherboard. "That's it!" I exclaimed with my mouth still mostly full.

Cyrus wiped the mayo that I'd spit off his shirt. "What's it?"

Cyrus shook his head and said, "No, I have some things to work on."

Mom looked over at him. "Like what? I'm away at a conference. Are you going into the lab on your own?"

"No. I have school work to do. Uh, an essay for English. I asked for extra credit." Cyrus was obviously lying, but this news put a huge smile on my mom's face.

"Did you hear that, Nathaniel? Cyrus asked for extra work. What a model student you are." My mom patted his knee proudly.

My dad's mouth twisted up like he'd just eaten something sour. He was trying to keep his comments to himself. "Yes, that's nice. Shawn, maybe you should do that, too."

I rolled my eyes, ready to expose Cyrus's lie, until I saw his face. His eyes were pleading with me. I quickly figured out that Cyrus must be using the time alone with Dad to work on his plan. "Ha, yeah. Maybe I should." I slunk down in my seat, not wanting to commit to actually doing extra work.

"Well!" My mom clapped with delight. "What do you boys want to watch? What about that new sitcom about the two girls who live in New York City?"

Cyrus grabbed the remote from Mom's hand and said, "How about the show about the guy who backpacks across Europe and learns how to cook regional dishes along the way?"

I looked out of the corner of my eyes at my dad's reaction. His lips twitched a little, like he wanted to smile in agreement. Instead he coughed, "That sounds . . . educational."

Cyrus was good. He was very good. He was playing right into my father's love of cooking. I was beginning to get an idea of what Cyrus's plan might be.

CHAPTER 4

AS MY MOM RAN THROUGH HER CHECKLIST OF WHAT WE needed to remember while she was gone that weekend, I was busy enjoying my new freedom. I didn't listen, because I knew I could get the audio recording from Cyrus later if I needed it.

She pulled Cyrus aside as she was leaving and said, "Remember, tomorrow is the one-week deadline of the ultimatum Nathaniel gave us. If we bother him in any way or make life seem strange to him, you'll have to live at the lab. Are you sure everything is running smoothly? Your systems are calibrated and all warning alarms are on silent?"

Cyrus nodded and assured her, "Don't worry. I'm going to lay low, do some homework, and play with Scooter. It'll be fine. You have nothing to be worried about."

She laughed nervously. "Famous last words . . . " On her way to the door she kissed me on the head, said goodbye to Scooter, and hollered outside to my dad in his workshop. The cab honked in the driveway and she was gone in a matter of seconds.

"So really, what's the plan?" I asked as soon as the door closed.

Cyrus crossed his arms. "If I tell you, you have to promise to stay out of the way."

"Deal," I spit on my palm and reached out. Cyrus stared at my hand. "You're supposed to shake it."

"That's not sanitary." Cyrus stuck his hands in his pockets.

"Sheesh, you and Dad are more alike than you think. So, what's the big plan?"

Cyrus waved me over to look at the tablet built into his palm. "I'm going to put in a new refrigerator." He showed me the photo, smiling as he pointed out all the interesting features.

I shrugged. "Who cares about a fridge? How's that supposed to win my dad over? What about doing some cool stuff? Where's the wow-factor?"

"What is a wow-factor?" Cyrus asked.

"You know, like an old-fashioned soda fountain or an ice cream parlor in the corner, or the world's largest gumball machine. You need to think about the whole family when adding something cool to the kitchen. Maybe think about a total redo." I walked over to the coffee table and clicked on the TV. "Here, watch a few episodes of these home renovation shows and you'll see what I mean."

Cyrus sat down and was immediately interested in the kitchen demolition happening on TV.

"Okay, I'm going to play some basketball with James. I'll see you later, 'kay?" I grabbed my hoodie and opened the door. Cyrus didn't even hear me leave. I could practically hear the electrical connections in his head whirring with ideas.

An hour later Cyrus came outside. He watched James and me play for a while, but decided not to join in. He was busy scribbling notes on his tablet.

James's mom drove up and asked if we wanted to go get ice cream while she went to the grocery store. Cyrus jumped in the car with us and said, "Mrs. McClure, would you mind giving me a ride to the hardware store? Is it on your way?"

"What do you need at the hardware store?" I asked, wondering if he would reveal the new plans for the kitchen.

"Just a few odds and ends."

"How are you going to get home?" Mrs. McClure asked.

"I'll ride in the delivery truck."

"The delivery truck? Are you still planning on buying a new fridge?" I laughed.

Cyrus shrugged. "Yes, and a few other things."

"How are you going to buy stuff? Do you have money?"

Cyrus nodded. "Some allowance money."

I looked over at him. "You get an allowance?"

"Yeah, I do chores, too."

James laughed. "What does a robot need money for anyway? External keyboards and memory chips?" Unlike most of the kids at school who worshipped Cyrus and thought he was the best thing ever, James wasn't impressed. He thought Cyrus was weird.

"Tiny tranquilizers, actually," Cyrus replied. "Perfect for quieting nosey humans."

James gulped and stayed quiet for the rest of the ride.

———

Mrs. McClure dropped me off at home later that evening. As I walked through the front door I could hear what sounded like the buzz of a chain saw coming from the kitchen. "Cyrus?" I called. I heard a faint whimper and found Scooter trying to hide under the coffee table. Of course, he was too chunky to fit, so just his head was covered.

I pushed open the door to the kitchen and peeked inside. "What are you doing?" I cried over the sound of the table saw that was positioned where the breakfast counter used to be.

The buzzing stopped and Cyrus lifted the safety goggles he was wearing. "You were right. A new fridge wasn't enough. You're looking at a full kitchen remodel!"

"Where's everything else that used to be in here?" I

looked around at the empty space. It looked like Cyrus was assembling cabinets. They were dark stained wood, way nicer than the flimsy particle board cabinets we used to have.

"I got rid of everything." He nodded toward the outside.

I peeked out the window and saw a huge dumpster. "How did you get all this done already?" Cyrus had completely gutted the kitchen and started building new cabinets in the time it took Mrs. McClure to do her weekly grocery shopping.

"I have a double-speed function, but it only works in ten minute increments, so I don't overheat." Cyrus pulled down the goggles, ready to get back to work.

"So, has Dad been home yet? Does he know you're doing all this?"

"No, not exactly," Cyrus looked around and I was beginning to see a look of panic on his face.

"Wait. Does he know about this?"

Cyrus shook his head. "No, I thought I'd be able to finish the remodel before he got home from his afternoon golf game. But," Cyrus pointed to the boxes that once held the cabinets, "did you know they don't include words on instruction pages? Just pictures of smiling people assembling the product. It's impossible to know what they're actually doing. They're stick figures!"

I held up the paper and laughed. "Yeah, looks like a comic book."

"Well, I've been searching all my online resources and I finally found some printed instructions, but they're written in a rural dialect of German, so I'm not sure if I'm supposed to fasten the door hinge to the base of the shelf, or milk a baby goat while dancing like a chicken."

I laughed, thinking Cyrus had made a joke, but his serious face told me he wasn't kidding. "Wait, really?"

"I know it seems like common sense to you, but I

have to run everything through translation services and then filter to see what the most human like response is. It's all very complicated." He looked upset.

I picked up the directions again and said, "Okay, I'll work on building the cabinets, and you work on the appliances."

We hurried over the next two hours, thinking we could turn the kitchen into a high-end, fine-dining workspace that my dad would go crazy for. But we were wrong to think that we could do a job in two hours that normally took teams of people weeks or months. Even though Cyrus was a world-class robot, he had definitely messed up calculating this renovation. When we heard Dad pull into the driveway, we surveyed the work. I had finished building the frames to two cabinets and Cyrus had managed to install the new six-burner double oven.

"Maybe he won't notice?" Cyrus looked at me with a hopeful glimmer in his eye.

I wouldn't lie to my brother. "Naw, man. He'll definitely notice."

"You think he'll kick me out?"

I sucked in a breath and nodded. "Yeah, probably."

Cyrus closed his eyes for so long I thought he'd shut down. When he finally opened them again I could tell he was terrified. "I can't believe I was so foolish. I don't want to leave, Shawn."

I slapped him on the shoulder. "Don't worry, Cyrus. Mom and I won't let that happen. Just hang tight and I'll go distract him. Keep working, okay?"

Cyrus's shoulders slumped in defeat. I couldn't let my dad see the demolished kitchen.

CHAPTER 5

I BURST THROUGH THE DOOR INTO THE LIVING ROOM TRYING TO figure out a way to stall my dad so Cyrus could keep working. "Hey, Dad! I'm starving. Let's go get pizza. It's Sunday Funday at Pizzeria Italia. You love their mushroom sauce. We could go now!"

"Shawn, your mother is coming home tonight," he said, and switched the bag of groceries he was carrying from one arm to the other.

"Great! She likes pizza. We can bring her home a slice!" I walked by him and grabbed my sweatshirt hanging by the door. "If we go now we'll beat the rush!"

"What is going on with you, boy? I bought fresh lump crab to make your mother's favorite crab cakes. Now, put your sweatshirt away—in your room."

He started to walk toward the kitchen door.

"Dad! Wait!" I called.

He stopped and turned back. He was annoyed. "What is it, Shawn?"

"Can you come up to my room and take a look at my, uhm . . . window?"

"What's wrong with your window?" my dad asked, looking up toward my room. Dad didn't like to hear about anything that wasn't in working order.

"It's, uh, squeaky. Yeah, when I open it, it squeaks." I was convinced Dad believed my lie when he started to walk toward the stairs. But then, a crashing sound came from the kitchen.

"What was that?" My dad rushed through the

kitchen door, took one look around and dropped the groceries on the floor. He pointed to the door, the front door, and calmly said, "Out."

Cyrus's mouth hung open for a second like he wanted to explain, but then he dropped his head and walked by my dad. He opened the front door and stepped onto the porch.

I followed Cyrus outside and watched him tap on the mini-tablet built into his palm. "What are you doing?" I asked, looking over his shoulder.

He didn't look up at me. "I'm reviewing my actions over the last week to see where I went wrong. If I can pinpoint a moment in time when I made an error in judgment I can adjust my behavior accordingly in the future."

"No." I waved off his weird robot explanation. "What are you doing out here? You're not leaving are you?"

"It looks like I might be. But for now, I'm waiting

for your mom to get home. I don't want to risk getting her in trouble with the lab by just disappearing."

"Okay, I'm going to go talk to my dad. I'll explain things." I went back inside to find my dad. He was still standing in the same spot in the kitchen muttering to himself.

When he saw me he shook his head and said, "Tell me this was not your fault."

"No, it was all Cyrus," I said.

"I knew it! That robot can't be trusted. A robot living with a family. What was your mother thinking?"

"But Dad, when I say it was all him, I mean the good stuff. He did all this for you. He told me about your cooking classes in Italy and he wanted to redo the kitchen so you had fancy chef tools to work with."

My dad's faced lightened a little. "But how did he know about that?"

I shrugged. "He's a robot. That's what he does."

Dad looked closely at the oven. "Is that what I think

it is? That is a top of the line oven." He ran his fingers over the burners. "How did he afford all this?"

"He said he had an allowance. Why? Is that an expensive stove?"

"Uh, yeah. Like a ten-thousand-dollar stove." My dad turned and looked out the window. "I see what he was trying to do here, but this kitchen is a disaster. I can't believe what a mess he made. Did he get a permit?" Suddenly, my dad didn't seem so angry anymore.

I shrugged. "I don't know."

My dad let out a huge sigh and rubbed his face. "Go get Cyrus and send him in. I'd like to speak with him." Then he handed me some money. "Use the phone in Mom's office to call for pizza. I want her to have something to eat when she gets home."

I ran to the front door and stuck my head out and said, "Dad wants to see you in the kitchen."

Cyrus looked up from his tablet. "Is it bad?"

"I think you can save this. Work your robot magic!"

Cyrus hung his head and slowly trudged through the living room and into the kitchen. The only thing I heard was my dad asking, "What were you thinking?"

I waited outside for the pizza. I knew how much Dad could yell and I didn't want to make it worse on Cyrus by listening to the whole thing. As soon as I'd tipped the delivery driver, Mom's taxi turned the corner.

"Hi, sweetheart!" My mom kissed the top of my head after she got out of the cab. "Yum. Pizza! Let's go eat! Are your Dad and Cyrus inside?"

I scratched my head. "Yeah, about Dad and Cyrus . . . " I told her what had happened with the kitchen remodel and her face fell.

"Oh no," she moaned. "I need to get inside and help them work things out. This is not good at all. We're getting so close with Cyrus. So close!" She hurried through the door and dropped her bags on the couch.

I followed her into the kitchen. Neither my dad nor Cyrus was there. My mom stepped through the door into the back yard, only giving the demolished kitchen a quick glance.

"Nathaniel, honey?" She poked her head into my dad's workshop. He looked up from his workbench.

"Welcome home!" He went to the door to greet her.

Mom looked between Dad and Cyrus, "So . . . what's going on?"

"Did you see the kitchen?" Dad sounded like he was laughing rather than fuming.

"Yes, I did. Shawn told me Cyrus wanted to surprise you with a custom kitchen." Mom was trying to find out how angry Dad really was.

"Yep. It sure was a surprise!"

"A good surprise or a bad surprise?" Mom asked.

"Well, I don't think a kitchen renovation done without a city permit is a good thing. In fact, I think it's sort of illegal." Dad looked over at Cyrus. "Right?"

My mom protectively stepped between my dad and Cyrus. "Surely there's something we can do to get the right permits and then it's all okay, right?"

My dad nodded. "It's all okay. Cyrus and I were just going over the list of tools we'll need to finish the renovation. He's already filed for the permit online and he's going to cover the fees for being out of compliance. Once we get the okay, we'll work on the kitchen together."

"You will?" My mom and I both asked.

My dad laughed. "Don't be so surprised. What Cyrus did was poorly planned and executed, but he did it with a pure heart."

I snickered, "He doesn't have a heart, Dad. He's a robot."

My dad shrugged, "I think he's got a pretty big heart, to think of doing something like this for me." He looked at Cyrus and smiled. "Thank you, Cyrus."

Later that night, I sat on the couch with Cyrus

watching TV. "So, you obviously said all the right things to my dad. He's your biggest fan now," I joked as I switched the channel.

Cyrus shrugged. "I wanted to build him a new kitchen and I told him so. I don't think I did anything to deceive him."

"But you built the kitchen so he wouldn't want to get rid of you. So really, you built it for yourself."

"No, I wanted to build it to give your dad something he deserves. He's a good guy." Cyrus stood up. "I have to go do my weekly updates."

My mom was standing on the stairs when I turned got up to go to bed. "What were you two just talking about?"

"Nothing really, just why Cyrus wanted to build Dad the kitchen."

"And what did he say?" Mom asked curiously.

"Because Dad deserves it, whatever that means."

I passed her on the stairs, but she grabbed my arm lightly.

"He said that?" she asked, her eyes sparkling. I nodded and she grinned widely. "Do you know what that means?"

"That he's probably lying and just did it to save himself from having to live at the lab."

My mom was already halfway down the stairs headed for her office before turning back to me. "No Shawn, it means that he's developing compassion and empathy. Those are the most complex human emotions. This is huge."

I shrugged and went to brush my teeth before bed. When I got to my room Cyrus was sitting on my bed.

"Hey, thanks for helping earlier. Those cabinets you built turned out really nice." He looked up at me with a friendly smile.

"Thanks. It was actually kind of fun. I'm glad Dad is letting you stay," I said.

Cyrus nodded. "Me, too."

"So, what now?"

Cyrus shrugged. "Now I guess I'm allowed to mess up without Dad wanting to kick me out. I'm sort of like a real son."

I laughed. "Don't be so sure that's all it's cracked up to be. Wait, did you just call him Dad?"

"Yep. He asked me to while we were discussing environmentally friendly paint brands." Cyrus smiled. "It's cool, right?"

I bit the inside of my lip, not sure why I suddenly felt jealous. "Yeah, it's cool. Welcome to the family, bro."